Shivers™

LOST IN DREAMLAND

M. D. Spenser

Paradise Press, Inc.

Plantation, Florida

Published by Paradise Press, Inc. by arrangement with River Publishing, Inc. All
right, title and interest to the "SHIVERS" logo and design are owned by River
Publishing, Inc. No portion of the "SHIVERS" logo and design may be reproduced
in part or whole without prior written permission from River Publishing, Inc. An
application for a registered trademark of the "SHIVERS" logo and design is pend-
ing with the Federal Patent and Trademark office.

ISBN 1-57657-103-3

30622

EXCLUSIVE DISTRIBUTION BY PARADISE PRESS, INC.

Cover Design by George Paturzo

Cover Illustration by Eddie Roseboom

Printed in the U.S.A.

To Bill and Jeanette

<u>Chapter One</u>

They were lost. Hopelessly lost.

And without them, the Donovan family had no chance to get out!

"I've looked everywhere," Mr. Donovan complained. "I can't find the car keys, honey. I just can't find them!"

"Did you look in your pants pocket?" Mrs. Donovan asked.

"Yes, twice!" Mr. Donovan responded. "Where are they? They can't be lost!"

While their parents searched the hotel room again and again, Bill and Barbara fumed. They had already wasted half the day — their *first* day ever in Orlando! How could two adults be dumb enough to lose the keys to the rental car?

"*Daaad*!" Barbara whined. "We should have been in Dreamland by now. You've been looking for those keys for almost a half hour!"

"Yeah, come on, Dad. Let's forget the car and take the train to Dreamland," Bill suggested. "That'd be more fun anyway."

"We're not taking the train, Bill! I *have* to find those keys!" Mr. Donovan snapped. "Why don't you and your sister help me look instead of complaining?"

So the Donovan twins joined the search for the missing keys, doing their best to hide their frustration and disappointment.

After all, this was the vacation both of them had begged their parents to take for at least four years. They had wanted it so badly, and waited for it so long.

Dreamland!

The biggest, newest, most popular, most realistic theme park in Orlando! Dreamland made Disney World seem like kiddie stuff, like virtual reality games compared to Monopoly.

The older theme park was still OK — pleasant enough for *young* kids, the Donovan twins supposed.

But if Disney World was a day at the beach, Dreamland was a voyage across the sea, a ship that carried visitors to strange, exotic ports of call.

All the kids said so!

Everyone in the neighborhood who went to Dreamland returned raving about the place.

Dreamland had the world's scariest haunted house!

Dreamland had the world's wildest roller coaster space ride!

And best of all, Dreamland had the world's most lifelike animated robots!

That was Dreamland's most important advance over all the other theme parks — everything inside the rides and exhibits looked completely real.

It was weird, the kids all said. Kind of spooky.

On the jungle ride, the crocodiles and giraffes looked as if they were really alive. But they weren't.

They were just fakes like every theme park had, doing the same thing over and over — the crocodiles biting at the canoes that passed by, and the giraffes reaching up to nibble tree leaves.

They just didn't look fake. Not at all!

On the pirate ride, all the bad guys appeared so real, slashing with their swords and drinking their rum, singing and dancing and fighting. Amazing!

But all of them were just animated, electronic models. Robots.

It was that way on every ride and in every exhibit at Dreamland. Totally realistic animals and people. As if they were made from real flesh and bone and blood.

No one knew how the technical wizards at Dreamland did it. That was their great secret — and the main reason for Dreamland's huge success.

Bill and Barbara and their parents were still hunting for the car keys when suddenly Mrs. Donovan spotted them — in the hotel waste basket!

"How did they get in there?" Mrs. Donovan scolded her husband. "Harry, I've told you a hundred times to take better care of your keys!"

"Yes, yes, yes, yes," Mr. Donovan answered. "I know, dear. I know. You never lose anything, do you? Well, I put them on the dresser and obviously they fell in the wastebasket somehow. It's not my fault."

"Who cares whose fault it is," Bill interrupted. "We've got the keys. Can't we get going now? It's almost noon already!"

"Yeah, you guys. Stop arguing and let's get to Dreamland," Barbara chimed in. "All the rides are going to be crowded by the time we get there. Let's go!"

And so, without any more argument, the Donovan family piled into the four-door rental car and headed off to Dreamland.

As they drove through the town of Kissimmee, past all the tacky neon signs for motels and restaurants, the twins watched eagerly for the city limits of Orlando.

Orlando!

The name sounded magical to the Donovan

children.

To them, Orlando was a combination of Christmas and the last day of school — about as close to kid heaven as anything could be.

And finally they were there. The sign said so.

"Look, Mom, we're in Orlando!" Barbara yelled. "I can't believe it!"

"Wow, we're really here!" Bill said. "This is gonna be great!"

"Yes, we're here. Now quiet down, you two," Mr. Donovan said. "You've done nothing but talk since we got in the car. We'll be in Dreamland in just a few minutes. I know you're excited, kids. But try to be a little quieter, will you, please? This traffic is terrible and I'm not sure where I'm going."

The Donovan twins looked at each other, grinned, and giggled — and said very little all the way to the grand golden entrance of Dreamland, which turned out to be a massive gate monitored by four guards on horseback.

The guards wore tall gold helmets and bright blue uniforms, and rode their horses proudly. Each guard approached one car at a time, leaning down to take the entrance tickets and ask the last names of Dreamland's new visitors.

"Lucky we got advance tickets. This is the gate for people who already bought theirs," Mr. Donovan said. "We get special treatment, I guess."

Indeed they did receive special treatment!

As the guard took their tickets, he announced each family as if they were guests at a royal ball.

"The Donovan family!" one guard called out loudly.

With that announcement, the huge gate swung open. Mr. Donovan drove into Dreamland as youthful trumpeters blared a welcome from both sides of the road.

"You know what I just realized? Those guards taking tickets weren't *real*!" Mr. Donovan said in amazement. "They were just dummies! Robots! So were the horses! These trumpeters are fake, too! See, you can tell by the way they all move so perfectly together. That's incredible!"

"How do they do that?" Mrs. Donovan

asked. "I can't understand how they make them look so believable."

"Wow, is that cool!" Bill exclaimed. "Is this the greatest place or what?"

"I can't wait to send my friends a post card," Barbara said.

The Donovans drove alongside African plains teeming with lifelike zebras and lions and elephants, all fake. The family saw a Civil War battle fought by electronic soldiers who looked very angry and very real.

They drove beside a large herd of buffalo stomping through the prairie of the Old West. They knew that every animal was nothing but plastic stretched over a bunch of wires and circuits. But to Bill and Barbara, those buffalo looked as real as their parents sitting in the front of the rental car.

And they saw all of this magic just on the drive to the parking lot!

What a place, Bill and Barbara both thought. All the kids were right.

Then, in an instant, the twins feared they

would never live to see any more of this incredible theme park!

Mr. Donovan was driving slowly as he approached a steep dip in the road. The street plunged abruptly, then turned so sharply that none of the family could see around the corner.

Until it was too late!

At the bottom of the dip, as the road ahead came into view again, the Donovans saw an enormous truck bearing down on them!

It was an eighteen-wheel tractor-trailer that looked like it was moving at top speed, probably a hundred miles an hour, or faster!

The truck's front bumper was only inches away from the Donovans' rental car.

Some maniac was going the wrong way on a one-way street!

The twins screamed!

"Aaaaaaaaagh!"

Before they ever enjoyed a single ride at the

park, the entire Donovan family was going to be squashed by an insane trucker who had run amok at Dreamland!

<u>Chapter Two</u>

"Hold on, kids!" Mr. Donovan yelled.

"Dad, look out!" Bill screamed.

"Daddy, *stop*!" Barbara hollered.

But Mrs. Donovan — well, she must have been hysterical! Because she started to laugh as the truck barreled toward their car!

"Ha, ha, heee, heeee," Mrs. Donovan giggled, her hand over her mouth.

Then the strangest thing happened — the Donovans' car passed right *through* the huge truck, as if the tractor-trailer were a ghost.

Mr. Donovan and Mrs. Donovan then dissolved into gales of laughter, slapping their legs and snorting through their noses.

"Ha, ha! I'm sorry, kids! It's all just a joke,"

Mr. Donovan chuckled. "When I bought our tickets, they told me what to expect from the fake truck — and I let your mother in on the secret. It's just one of the ways Dreamland gives you kids a thrill."

"Huh? I don't get it," Barbara said, annoyed.

"Me either! What happened to the truck that almost hit us? Where did it go?" Bill asked irritably.

"There *was* no truck, kids!" Mrs. Donovan laughed.

"It was just a hologram," Mr. Donovan explained. "You know, a laser image that looks three-dimensional but isn't really there. The truck looked real — but it was just a picture made from light. So we just drove right through it."

"Wow, was that cool! Man, this is an unbelievable theme park," Bill said enthusiastically.

"Well, yeah, I guess it is," Barbara said, somewhat less impressed. "But I was really scared. I thought we all were going to die in a horrible car crash. That's not funny!"

"It's supposed to scare you, Babs," Bill said, using the nickname Barbara hated most. "That's what makes it fun! Don't be such a baby."

"I'm not a baby! I just don't think it's funny to frighten people out of their wits, is all," Barbara responded. "And don't call me 'Babs!' "

The twins were twelve years old and, despite occasional bickering, were as close as a brother and sister could be. They loved each other very much, though neither ever expressed those feelings directly to the other.

Somehow they just knew it, without having to say the words.

Many things were like that for them — they simply understood each other, almost as if the brother could read the mind of his sister and the sister could read the mind of her brother.

They had been born in Detroit, eleven minutes apart, on a cold December day.

Since then, they had rarely been separated for more than a few hours.

They were intelligent children who usually did well in school, loved to read, and played in the school band. Bill performed wonderfully on the oboe, Barbara just as well on the clarinet, the oboe's sister instrument.

They even looked alike.

Both had curly dark hair, with thick eyebrows and prominent cheekbones. Both were slim and a little short for their age. Both wore metal-frame glasses on their rather long noses.

Large noses ran in their father's family, judging from old photographs of Grandpa and Great-Grandpa Donovan. No one ever called their father's nose small, either.

Sometimes other kids teased Bill or Barbara about their noses — though never when the twins were together. They always stuck up for each other, cleverly shooting down anyone who dared criticize their noses or anything else.

Around school the Donovans were known as brains, but witty brains who didn't shrink from an argument.

Bill was bolder, Barbara a bit more timid. Together they were a force no one dared challenge to a battle of wits.

"Here we are, kids!" Mr. Donovan announced cheerily. "Let's hop on the Bullet Train for Dreamland!"

The family parked their car in the vast lot, and everyone noted the space number: PH36. If anyone got separated from the others, Mr. Donovan said, the whole family would meet at that parking space. Remember, he repeated: PH36.

The Bullet Train carried the Donovans and hundreds of other eager families to Dreamland at incredible speeds — nearly 200 miles an hour. It felt like sitting inside a rocket that never left earth.

In less than five minutes, everyone got off in the center of Dreamland.

"Look, there's the Man in the Moon," Barbara shouted, pointing at the best-known symbol of Dreamland.

The Man in the Moon was a huge fake moon that seemed to hang in mid-air over the park, its gray craters and canyons clearly visible. Visitors rode individual space ships that flew *inside* this moon, tearing around at blinding speeds, twisting up and down, right and left, forward and backward.

Friends had told the twins that thousands of lasers bending this way and that way inside the ride made it look as if you were traveling faster than light.

"Please, Dad, let's go there first! Please, please," Bill begged.

"Yeah, come on, Mom! Let's go to the Man in the Moon! Please," Barbara said.

The line looked a mile long and three miles wide. But, reluctantly, Mr. and Mrs. Donovan agreed to start with the Man in the Moon. It was supposed to be one of Dreamland's best rides.

After all, it wasn't the twins' fault that they had arrived so late, Mrs. Donovan reminded her husband. He just sighed and waved toward the Man in the Moon, and immediately Bill and Barbara took off, running toward the entrance.

As they raced toward the "launching pad" for the space ships, a man stepped out of the crowd and stopped them.

A large man wearing a mask!

And holding a gun!

He was a robber!

"Hold it right there, kids!" he demanded in a low grumble of a voice. "Your money or your lives!"

Bill glanced back desperately at his parents. Mr. and Mrs. Donovan were looking casually around the park as they walked toward the Man in the Moon entrance. They had not noticed the robber — and they were too far away to help their children now anyway.

"Come on! Come on! Hurry it up!" the robber yelled. "Your money or your lives! Take your pick, kids!"

Bill and Barbara looked at each other, shrugging their shoulders helplessly.

"W-we don't, uh, have any money," Bill said. "Our parents have it. But if you'll just, uh, w-wait, I'll ask my dad . . . "

"No waiting! You don't have any money to give me, right?" the robber scowled. "OK, kiddies! I said your money or your lives. So now I guess I'm gonna have to take your lives!"

Chapter Three

Bill and Barbara trembled.

Was a gunman really going to murder them in the middle of Dreamland?

Why didn't someone come to their rescue?

How could such an awful thing happen at such a well-run, popular theme park?

The robber-killer stuck out his long, gray gun and pulled the trigger — and they heard a loud explosion!

But instead of a bullet, a little flag popped out of the barrel! A flag that said, "Fooled You!"

And that was when Bill understood something: The robber wasn't real! No more real than the guards at the front gate or the horses or the trumpeters.

No more real than the Civil War soldiers or the buffalo or the tractor-trailer.

It was just another amazing Dreamland fantasy — somehow brought to life by the wizardry of electronic animation.

"Cool!" Bill grinned.

"Rotten!" Barbara frowned, rolling her eyes. "I hope Dreamland isn't going to be doing stuff like this to us all the time! I don't like being scared by something that seems so real!"

"Aw, don't be a scaredy-cat! Come on, Babs! Let's go to the Man in the Moon!" Bill said, starting to run.

"Hey, wait up, Bill! And stop calling me 'Babs!' " Barbara called after him.

The twins found a place in the monstrous line and waited as their parents finally joined them.

"Mom, did you see what happened back there?" Barbara complained. "They had this fake robber come out and he looked really real and everything! And he threatened to kill us, Mom! I don't think I like this place as much as I expected to!"

"Honey, don't let it upset you so much! These things are all just part of the fun here," Mrs. Donovan replied. "You can't take everything that happens in Dreamland so seriously."

"That's right, darling," Mr. Donovan said. "It's all a big game here, Barbara. You learn that in Dreamland, seeing *isn't* believing! This is a place where you can't trust your own eyes!"

"I think it's *cooool*," Bill said.

The line wound around and around in large circles. An hour later, the Donovans seemed hardly any closer to the entrance.

The crowd that waited outside the launching pad was enormous. Bill and Barbara had to stand in line almost another hour before they were finally strapped into their private space ships, ready to blast off toward the giant moon that hovered over Dreamland.

Mrs. Donovan decided to avoid this particular ride, not wanting to lose her breakfast. Mr. Donovan did not seem eager for an interstellar journey either, even though their children urged them to blast off with everyone else.

"Come on, you guys! You *have* to go!" Bill said. "You can't stand in line for two hours, then chicken out at the last minute."

"Yeah, come on Mom and Dad! Please?" Barbara begged. "If I'm not too scared to go on this ride, you guys shouldn't be scared either."

"Harry, you go ahead, if you want to be a kid again. I don't mind," Mrs. Donovan had told her husband. "But not me. I'll just get sick and feel dizzy the rest of the day."

"No, I'll stay with you, honey," Mr. Donovan had answered, sounding none too disappointed. "Sorry, kids. I'd like to go, of course. But, well, I don't want to leave your mother all alone in this big park."

After almost two hours of waiting, they were ready. At least the ride was worth the wait! It was worth every minute they had spent in line, Bill and Barbara thought.

The experience was astonishing! Like nothing else they had ever seen.

Each rocket zoomed in wild, gut-wrenching turns through galaxies of stars, past planets, into asteroid showers, all at warp speeds.

It looked and felt incredibly real, like everything in Dreamland.

The rockets roared past colonies of space explorers who had settled on distant worlds, people whose lifelike faces were clearly visible through their helmets, smiling and laughing as their fellow earthlings approached.

Space-walking astronauts tethered to orbiting crafts waved happily as the twins' rockets raced through the universe inside The Man in the Moon.

After the ride ended, the twins said they were hungry — even after all those stomach-turning spins and dives in their space ships.

The family picked one of Dreamland's many restaurants and ate a delicious meal of grilled chicken and corn bread, collard greens and cole slaw — real southern barbecue.

And all of it was served by robots that appeared just like humans. Most of the waiters and waitresses looked like kids about their own age, kids who talked and walked and filled orders as if they were real children.

Just unbelievable, the Donovans marveled.

It would have been a terrific lunch, too. The food was great, the atmosphere inside the barbecue restaurant was authentic — and the help, of course, was very friendly, if only made of plastic skin and silver circuitry.

But something happened that frightened Bill Donovan more than he had ever been frightened before.

And it panicked the rest of his family, too.

Bill began to choke on a large piece of chicken.

He coughed and gagged, then suddenly couldn't breathe at all!

"Son, are you OK?" Mr. Donovan asked, jumping up. "Are you all right, Bill? Talk to me, son!"

Bill couldn't say a word. The piece of food had lodged firmly in his windpipe. He couldn't get even a wisp of air in or out of his lungs.

No one in the family knew what to do.

They had never taken a course that showed them how to deal with emergencies of that kind, though Mrs. Donovan had wanted to sign up for such a class at the Red Cross.

Now she wished desperately that she had done it!

Without any idea how to help, Mr. Donovan did the worst thing — he slapped Bill hard on the back. That forced the piece of chicken further down Bill's windpipe.

Bill could feel himself turning blue from lack of air. He could feel the food jammed down his throat, like a cork shoved into the neck of a bottle.

He could feel the life beginning to drain out of his body.

Unless something happened, unless someone took action to save him quickly — *very* quickly — Bill Donovan was going to choke to death in a

Dreamland barbecue restaurant.

And there was nothing his family could do to save him!

Chapter Four

One of the robot waiters saw what was happening.

At once, he called out for help.

"Choking!" he shouted.

Within seconds, the door to the kitchen burst open and a large man wearing a chef's hat ran out. Without a word, he reached his arms around Bill from behind, grabbing him just below the rib cage and forcefully pushing a fist into his abdomen.

The chunk of chicken flew out of Bill's mouth and landed on the table in front of him.

He could breathe again!

As Bill gasped for air, his parents rose and thanked the chef profusely for saving their son.

"Oh, thank you! Thank you, thank you!" Mrs.

Donovan said. "I can't thank you enough for what you did!"

"I don't know what to say to you, sir. You saved our boy's life!" Mr. Donovan said, shaking the chef's hand. Suddenly, an odd expression came over Mr. Donovan's face. "Uh, well, thanks very much for that, uh, I guess."

"It was nothing, folks. Glad to do it," the chef said, smiling and turning to Bill. "Now you be more careful next time, son. Chew your food before swallowing it, OK? And all of you enjoy your stay at Dreamland."

The chef returned to the kitchen. Mrs. Donovan's complexion turned red as she began to scold her husband.

"Why did you get that funny look on your face when you thanked that man?" she asked angrily. "He'll think you didn't appreciate what he did to save Bill. How could you treat him so rudely?"

"I appreciate it all right," Mr. Donovan said uncomfortably. "It's just that I didn't know what to say after I realized . . . well . . . "

"Realized *what*?" Mrs. Donovan asked.

"Realized that the chef wasn't a real man. He was fake. A robot like all the others," Mr. Donovan replied. "I was shocked when I shook his hand. It was all cold and hard. Shaking his hands was like shaking hands with a plastic jug. I didn't know what to say. I felt silly thanking a machine."

"A *machine*!" said Bill, even more shocked than his father. "How could that be? You mean, they have machines trained to give the Hemlock Maneuver or whatever it is?"

"*Heimlich* maneuver, dopey," Barbara said. "That's what they call it when you force air out of someone's chest to get food unstuck. I'd have tried it myself only they haven't taught us the right way to do it in school yet."

"Whatever, Babs. I don't care what it's called. But it just seems so weird that Dreamland wouldn't have a real person working in the restaurant who knew how to do that," Bill said, scratching his head.

"I agree with you, Bill," Mr. Donovan said.

"It's very odd. And it's just as strange that he was wearing a chef's hat! Is he really the chef here?"

"I suppose he must be, don't you think?" Mrs. Donovan said. "Why else would he wear that hat — especially if he's not visible to the public most of the time? He must do the cooking."

"How could they have robots make the food here?" Barbara said. "Doesn't it require *people* to do something as creative as cooking?"

"It kind of gives me the creeps," Bill said, looking at his food.

"Yes, it is very strange. To rely on robots to cook the food as well as serve it," Mrs. Donovan said. "And it's especially strange to depend on a machine for something as critical as saving children from choking to death."

Mr. Donovan paused to think. Then he shook his head, as if to dismiss his own fears.

"Well anyway, the important thing is Dreamland had someone — uh, some*thing* — here to save people from choking," he said. "And it worked. I guess we should just be happy about that. And the food was good. I don't know why it makes us all so uncomfortable to think of machines doing things for us. It's the way of the future. I guess we're just not used to it."

"I guess that's it," Mrs. Donovan agreed.

"Yeah, I guess so," Barbara said.

"No, I guess *not*," Bill argued. "It's not that we're uncomfortable with the idea of machines doing these things, Dad. It's that machines aren't supposed to be so advanced that they *can* do these things! How is this even possible? How does Dreamland get machines to act just like people?"

"Yeah, that's a good question," Barbara said.

"Technology isn't *that* miraculous yet. How can any of this really *be*?" Bill asked.

His question hung in the air like a kite dangling helplessly from a high electric line.

No one in the Donovan family had the slightest idea how to begin answering it.

Chapter Five

"Come on, you guys!" Bill called to his family. "Hurry up! It's right over here! Come on, come on! Hurry!"

The Donovan family had left the restaurant and walked across half of Dreamland, much to Bill's irritation. He had wanted to run.

The next stop on the Donovans' agenda was the ride Bill had anticipated most eagerly — The Haunting House.

It was based on a famous story about two girls who moved with their family into a strange, old house — not a haunted house but a *haunting* house! The place was possessed by an evil spirit that made it hate the residents, trying to kill them.

This was the coolest, scariest, most realistic

of all the rides in Dreamland, the guys at school had told Bill.

Even the outside of the ride was spooky, Bill's friends had said.

And so it was.

When the Donovans arrived, there was no waiting line at all. This time, their luck was good. They passed through a large archway that marked the entrance to the ride — and suddenly, magically, daytime turned to night.

The rickety, two-story house appeared before them, framed by stars with the huge Dreamland moon hovering mysteriously in the background. Bizarre eyes peered from the metal mailbox out front and large black birds shrieked through the darkened sky.

The door was open.

"Enter!" a booming voice commanded.

The Donovans joined several other families, all of whom laughed and snickered as they entered what was said to be the most terrifying ride in Dreamland. Everyone tried to act brave, but most of them looked pretty nervous.

Bill and Barbara looked at each other, and each knew what the other was thinking: This was going to be *really* creepy.

Their group was met at the door by two sisters, Caitlin and Lynne, who guided their guests into the front hall.

Suddenly, one by one, all by themselves, the doors and windows in the old house closed and the heavy metal locks slammed shut: *Gggwwaaccckk! Gggwwaaccckk! Gggwwaaccckk!*

They were trapped inside!

Caitlin and Lynne — who were, of course, just machines, like practically everyone else at Dreamland — let out a very believable shriek.

Then they raced along the creaky wooden floors toward the basement, shouting at the top of their lungs: *"Run for your lives, everyone! Take cover wherever you can! You're all on your own! Just try to get out of this haunting house alive!"*

So *that* was how the ride would be — not a ride at all!

Visitors were free to wander into any part of the haunting house, to go and come as they pleased — all while trying to avoid the attacks of the fierce old home.

Each room held a new, terrifying surprise.

The Donovan family entered the kitchen. Drawers and cabinets began to open and close by themselves. A moment later, a heavy wooden drawer in the kitchen counter exploded toward them like a missile.

And this missile was aimed straight at Barbara's brains!

"Duck, Barbara!" Bill yelled.

She tried to duck — but too late!

The drawer rammed right into her head — and then, incredibly, right *through* her head, just as a ghost would pass through a brick wall.

The drawer was just another clever Dreamland trick, another hologram like the tractor-trailer truck. It wasn't real.

"Ha!" Bill laughed, pointing at Barbara. "They got ya! Ha, ha, ha!"

"Yeah, well, you thought it was real, too, smart guy!" Barbara shot back.

"Come on, kids," Mr. Donovan said, excitedly. He seemed to enjoy the haunting house as much as his children did. "Let's go upstairs and see if we can find a way out of here alive!"

Mr. and Mrs. Donovan and the twins raced through the menacing house. Without warning, all the lights went out!

They stood in total blackness. Bill put his hand right in front of his face, but could not see it.

Then, mysteriously, small candles lighted themselves.

The Donovans hurried up the steps, which creaked and groaned with every footfall, and saw an old man motioning toward a place marked "Lynne's room."

"OK, let's see what's in there," Mr. Donovan said with a laugh. "Maybe this gentleman knows something we don't."

As they all rushed into Lynne's room, Mr. Donovan wondered: Was that old guy real? Or was he just another lifelike fake, a robot? He looked again.

The old man was gone.

It didn't matter. This was fun. No wonder kids loved Dreamland so much!

Inside Lynne's room, three or four adults and a few kids milled around. Some laughed. Others wore worried looks.

"Look, a secret tunnel!" one of the mothers said, pointing into Lynne's closet. "Maybe one of the kids should go into it to see if there's a way out of this house. That tunnel's way too small for the grown-ups."

Each of the kids thought this was a great idea — as long as he or she was chosen as the one to go.

"Me! Oh, let me! Mom, can I go?" all the kids yelled, raising their hands and jumping up and down.

Bill and Barbara yelled and waved and jumped, too. They looked at each other and wondered what scary, wonderful things would await the person who ventured into that tunnel.

"Hey, why don't we send these *two* kids into the tunnel?" a man suggested, pointing at Bill and Barbara. "They look like twins! That way two kids get to go instead of just one. Besides, we could use some twins."

Bill and Barbara looked at their parents. Their parents looked at each other.

"Let them have fun," Mr. Donovan said.

"Why not? Everything here is safe," Mrs. Donovan said. "It's all fantasy."

The twins kissed their mother good-bye: "We may never see you again," Bill joked. Everyone laughed.

Bill and Barbara bent down and crawled on their hands and knees into the tiny, black tunnel.

"Come on, Babs! Move faster than that or we'll never get anywhere," Bill called.

"I'm crawling as fast as I can," Barbara said. "And stop calling me 'Babs' or I'm going to sock you good!"

Their voices echoed back along the tunnel to Mr. and Mrs. Donovan, who smiled at each other.

"I guess we'll all have to find our own way out now," Mrs. Donovan said. "We'll meet up with the kids outside, I guess."

"You folks go ahead," said a man. "We'll just stay here for a while and see what they find in the tunnel. Go on ahead without us. And just enjoy your stay at Dreamland."

Enjoy your stay at Dreamland.

That sounded familiar, Mr. Donovan thought. Someone else had said the same thing not long ago, though he couldn't remember exactly who it was.

As he and his wife walked down the creaking stairs together, Mr. Donovan found himself wondering.

Were the people in Lynne's room real? Or were they just robots?

He had not seen them clearly in the dim and wavering candlelight.

Then he recalled something one of those people had said just before Bill and Barbara crawled into the tunnel — something that now seemed very, very odd.

A man in Lynne's room had said, "Besides, we could use some twins."

What in the world could he possibly have meant by that, Mr. Donovan wondered uneasily.

We could *use* some *twins*?

What could anyone possibly have meant by such a strange comment?

Chapter Six

Bill and Barbara crawled on and on and on through the black tunnel.

They could see nothing in front of them, nothing behind them.

Not even each other.

This Dreamland fantasy-terror was getting tiresome!

Why didn't something happen, Bill wondered. Some great, horrible, frightening thing?

Bill recalled that in the famous Haunting House tale, Lynne, who was nine, crawled into the tunnel in her room — where she was overcome by cockroaches.

And didn't the tunnel start to squeeze shut around her, too?

Where were the fake bugs? Why wasn't anything going on?

Maybe something was broken, Bill thought.

Barbara was thinking the same thing. But she was less eager than Bill to be covered by cockroaches, even fake ones. Certainly, she felt as impatient as her brother with this fake horror, a horror that was more tedious than terrible.

"What's going on, Bill? We're not getting anywhere," Barbara said. "How long are we going to have to crawl around in here?"

"I know. It's weird, isn't it?" he responded. "I wish we'd just stayed with Mom and Dad. Probably all sorts of cool stuff is happening to them inside the different rooms of the house."

"Do you think we should keep going or turn back?" Barbara asked.

"We *have* to keep going, Barbara," Bill answered. "We don't have enough space to turn around. And we can't crawl backwards all the way back to Lynne's room. Let's just keep moving. I can't wait to get out of here."

"I agree," Barbara said. "This is getting really bad, you know? It's hot in here and it's tiring and it's boring as anything! I want to get out and go to the next ride."

The twins crawled on and on, talking to keep their spirits up. They tried hard to make each other feel better in this black, endless hole.

"What ride do you want to go to next?" Bill asked. "The Haunting House was my choice. Next we should go to a ride you want to visit."

"I want to go to The Doll House! That's supposed to be so great," Barbara said immediately. "All my friends who've been to Dreamland say it's their favorite."

"Dolls! Yuck!" Bill said. But he was laughing. "That sounds so dull to me. But guess I ought to be a good sport and go there with you."

"You might even like it," Barbara said, wiping dust from her mouth as she crawled along. "You sit in this wooden sailing ship and you cruise to ports all over the world. The places look just like the real thing — you know, like you're really on a beach in

Tahiti or wherever. And the dolls look just like the real people from those countries. They sing and dance and walk and talk, just like the real people."

"Just like everybody at Dreamland walks and talks like real people. Even though they're not," Bill said. "What an amazing place this is. I just can't figure out how they do it."

The twins kept talking — and they kept crawling. Nothing changed in the tunnel, neither for the better nor for the worse.

The tunnel didn't get any larger, and it didn't get any smaller. It didn't get any lighter and it couldn't possibly get any darker.

There was no sound, except for the twins' voices accompanied by the squeaking of their hands and dragging of their feet as they crawled and crawled and crawled.

Then, suddenly, something in the tunnel finally did change.

They heard a noise. An eerie, spooky, haunting type of noise!

It was a low howl, a wail from somewhere far

off inside the tunnel:

Weeeooooaaawww!

The howl echoed from so far in front of them in the tunnel that the twins feared they might have to crawl another mile to get out.

That thought stopped them in their tracks.

The idea that they still had so much farther to go was more upsetting to Bill and Barbara than the frightening yell itself.

After all, they were in a Dreamland spook house. They *expected* weird things to happen. They just didn't expect to crawl through the darkness for hours, inside a tunnel that seemed like anything but fun.

"Bill, I don't know how much longer I can go on like this," Barbara complained. "My hands and knees are killing me!"

"I know, Barbara. Mine, too!" Bill said. "But I don't know what else we can do except keep going. I'm sorry we got into this mess. But all we can do is crawl out and never come back to this Haunting House again."

But Bill was wrong. They couldn't keep going at all.

Because they had stopped at exactly the right place — which is to say, at exactly the *wrong* place for them!

The strange howl was *supposed* to make them stop crawling, just as it did.

Now, a heavy steel door slammed shut in front of Barbara!

And a heavy steel door slammed shut behind Bill!

"*Aaaaaaahh!*" Barbara screamed. "Bill, the tunnel in front of me is closed! Quick, crawl backwards!"

"I can't, Barbara!" Bill yelled. "A huge piece of metal just closed behind me! We're stuck here!"

"*Heeeellpp!*" Barbara shouted. "Someone help us! We're stuck in the tunnel!"

"*Heeelllllpp!*" Bill yelled. "Can anyone hear us? We're trapped inside the tunnel! Someone get us out!"

But no one answered.

And no one heard.

And no one got them out.

The Donovan twins were trapped in The Haunting House!

And the air inside their tiny, sealed space was getting very thin — and very hard to breathe!

Chapter Seven

The twins coughed and sputtered.

Aaaachk! Aaaachk! Pheeewwwth!

They wheezed and gasped.

Wwwhhuuuzzz! Wwwhhuuuzzz! Yyyuuuuuhh!

"Bill, I can — *Wwwhhuuuzzz! Aaaachk!* — hardly breathe," Barbara moaned. "What's happening? I'm feeling so hot. Kind of lightheaded, too."

"These metal doors — *Pheeewwwth! Pheeewwwth!* — must have sealed us in an airtight space, Barbara," Bill said. "We're not getting any oxygen in here. We should stop talking and try to breathe slowly. *Very* slowly!"

"But Bill, if we're — *Yyyuuuuuhh! Yyyuuuuuhh!* — in a sealed space, we're going to suffocate," Barbara said. Every word required an effort. "We'll die unless we can find a way to make a hole and let air in!"

"Shhhh! Barbara, try to breathe slowly. And don't talk!" Bill instructed. "I'll try to hold my breath as much as I can while I yell for help!"

Barbara, gasping for air, tried her best to breathe slowly. Bill struggled to hold each breath he took, letting the air out gradually while pounding on the tunnel and yelling as loudly as he could.

"*Heeeeelllp*! *Heeelllpp*!" he shouted. "We're trapped in the tunnel! We can't breathe! *Heeeeelllpp*!"

Neither Bill nor Barbara heard any response, nothing to indicate that help was on the way.

It looked hopeless.

There was little air left in their tiny, black cubicle.

And very little time left for them to live — unless something saved them in the next few seconds.

No oxygen remained. None.

The twins slumped inside the tunnel, collapsing to the floor.

The end was near.

Then, in an instant, they felt a huge rush of fresh air flooding the tunnel.

They were breathing again! Breathing freely and deeply!

Unfortunately, at the same moment they also were falling fast down a deep dark hole!

The steel plates that had sealed them in the tunnel had trapped them directly over a trap door.

And the trap door had opened!

They tumbled screaming through the air as they toppled from the second story of the rickety house!

"Aaaaaaaaahhh!" yelled Bill.

"Aaaaaaaahhhh!" Barbara screamed.

And as they plummeted earthward, Bill and Barbara knew they were hurtling to their deaths!

Chapter Eight

Their fall seemed to go on forever.

It was as if they fell in slow motion, watching themselves turning end over end as they dropped toward destruction.

At long last, they hit bottom!

Pooooooff!

Pooooooff!

But they did not smash into a hardwood floor or some patch of concrete or even a patch of earth.

Instead, the Donovans landed squarely on two enormous down pillows, plopping onto the cushions quietly and safely.

They hadn't been squished! They had lived, after all!

But soon, they would almost wish they

hadn't.

It wasn't so bad at first. Bill and Barbara were mostly just confused.

They found themselves in a dark, dank room, a place with no lights and a smell that reminded them of dead rats.

"Are you OK, Bill?" Barbara asked, standing up and brushing herself off. "I don't think I'm hurt anywhere."

"Yeah, I'm fine, too. It was a good thing these pillows were here, though," Bill answered, dusting off his pants. "Where *are* we anyway?"

"This must be a storage room beneath The Haunting House," Barbara said. "Probably some place where the Dreamland people keep props for the house or something. There has to be a way out. Let's get away from here. It's spooky."

"OK, sure. Mom and Dad are probably waiting for us outside," Bill said. "They must be pretty worried."

The room was so dark that Bill and Barbara had a hard time seeing each other, much less finding the door to the outside. They stumbled through the blackness with their hands extended like blind people, feeling the walls for anything resembling a doorknob.

"I can't find anything. Can you?" Bill asked. "There must be some way to get out of this room. There has to be a door *somewhere*."

"No, I haven't found anything yet. All I feel is a cement wall, Bill," she replied. "How could the people who designed this place have been so stupid? How could they let tourists crawl into some tunnel that has a trap door in it that kids can fall through? They could be sued for negligence or something!"

"I don't get it, either, Barbara. It seems pretty weird. And pretty sloppy for a theme park that's as advanced as this one," Bill said, still feeling his way through the darkness. "I just wish I knew where we were. Obviously, we're below The Haunting House somewhere. But how far below? It seemed like we fell a long way. We must be someplace that's even below the basement. All I know for sure is that this room gives me the creeps."

"I was thinking the same thing. It's like a

dungeon in here," Barbara said. "It's one thing to be in some amusement house where the stuff is spooky but fake. But it's different to be in this room where things are spooky and real. I don't like it in here, Bill! I want Mom and Dad! I want to go back to our hotel room. And I'm not sure I ever want to see Dreamland again."

"I agree with you, sis. This place is a little too weird for me. Black tunnels and robot chefs and fake burglars and everything else," Bill said. "But we've got to find a door or a window or something — soon. We've been gone from Mom and Dad for a long time now. They may think we went out a different way, and maybe they won't wait outside the house much longer. Maybe they'll think we're lost."

"Yeah, we may have to go back by train to that parking space miles and miles away to meet up with them," Barbara said. "Space PH36. Remember?"

"Sure, I remember! Dad sure drummed it into our heads enough, didn't he?" Bill said. "Let's just stop talking and find a door. I feel like something bad is going to happen to us again if we don't get out of here soon!"

"I know, I know!" Barbara said. "I have exactly the same feeling, Bill!"

Just then, the Donovan twins heard rapid footsteps from across the room. They saw the beam of a flashlight pointed toward the cement floor.

Someone had found them! At last, some Dreamland employees were coming to rescue them and return them to their parents!

"Here they are, boys," a gruff male voice said. "Take 'em now and hold onto 'em!"

Bill and Barbara felt strong, hairy hands grabbing their arms from behind. And grabbing hard!

"Hey, what are you doing?" Bill asked angrily. "We're tourists here! Leave us alone!"

"Stop it, stop it!" Barbara shouted. "Our parents are waiting for us outside. We fell from the tunnel on the second floor! We're just tourists from Detroit! Stop hurting us!"

The strong, hairy hands squeezed tighter, pulling the twins' arms back so far that their shoulder blades almost touched each other.

"Shut up, you kids! Keep 'em quiet, will ya, boys?" the gruff voice said. "Don't take any back talk from these two! If they give you any trouble, tie 'em up!"

"OK, sure boss," said the man holding Barbara.

"Tie 'em up good and tight if you have to," the gruff voice said. "We don't want to lose these two! We can really use a good pair of twins!"

Chapter Nine

"Where are you taking us?" Bill demanded angrily. "Let us *go!*"

"Yeah, what do you think you're doing?" Barbara snapped at the two men. "You can't treat us like this! My father will have the police arrest all of you people before you can blink!"

The men laughed.

"Man, they're feisty, these two," one of the men commented. "And they like to talk."

"Yeah, they talk maybe *too* much," the other man said. "The boss told us to keep them shut up. He doesn't want trouble with them. We're supposed to watch these ones real good. They're kind of special because they're twins and all."

"Yeah, so *shut up, you two!*" the first man

yelled. "Or we're gonna gag you and tie you up with rope!"

Each man held on to one of the children with one hand. The men marched the Donovans quickly through the dark room, which was lighted now by a single flashlight beam cast toward the floor.

They already had walked a long way, with no end and no destination in sight.

The room was much larger than Bill and Barbara had imagined. This was no storage area.

The room now felt more like some old underground subway station. But why would Dreamland have an old subway station beneath the theme park?

It made no sense. No sense at all.

Where in the world were they, the twins wondered. Where in the world were they going?

Who was taking them there?

And most importantly, why?

After several more minutes of walking, Bill and Barbara spotted two tiny headlights in the distance.

The beams grew larger and brighter as the

headlights approached. At first, the Donovans thought a train was moving toward them through the underground station. Then it looked more like a bus.

But soon, a van sped up to their side. The driver slammed on the brakes. The van screeched to a stop.

"Get in, you two," one of the men ordered the twins. "And no trouble — from either of you!"

Bill opened the door and saw a rotund man with a heavy black beard and long black hair in one of the rear seats. The man motioned toward the empty seat in front of him.

"Climb in right there, kids!" he said, pointing. It was the man with the gruff voice! "Sit there quietly like good little twins — and maybe you won't get hurt!"

Bill and Barbara gulped and trembled, looking worriedly at each other. They wanted to run but knew better than to try. There was nothing at all they could do.

So they did just as they were told, clambering into the long seat in front of the bearded man, who slammed the van door shut.

A small man in the driver's seat jammed the transmission in gear and the van raced off, tires sliding and squealing.

"Where are you taking us, mister?" Bill asked the bearded man politely, hoping friendliness might help where anger had failed. "Maybe you and your friends were expecting someone else. If you would just drop us off outside The Haunting House, we'd really appreciate it. And so would our parents."

"Yes, our father the police officer would be very grateful to all of you gentlemen," Barbara chimed in, lying in an attempt to frighten the bearded man. Mr. Donovan really was a furniture salesman.

"It's clear to my brother and me that there's been some misunderstanding. You gentlemen obviously were expecting someone else in that room. So if you would just be kind enough to let us out, we'll go on our way. Dad will be very worried. I'm sure he probably has called his friends at the Orlando Police Department by now."

"That's right," Bill agreed. "He's a SWAT

team member from the Detroit police. And those guys know each other all around the country. So there may already be dozens of police officers searching everywhere for us."

The bearded man chuckled a deep, growling laugh that seemed more annoyed than amused.

"You twins really crack me up," he said gruffly. "Do you think I'm going to buy that load of bunk? Yeah, your daddy's a cop, right? Yeah, sure, I'll bet! Funny, it seems like every kid has a cop for a father — or at least a judge or an FBI guy or somebody like that. That's what they all say!"

Every kid, the twins thought. What did that mean?

Had these men done this same thing to other children before?

The van drove on and on, speeding through this underground station or tunnel or whatever it really was.

The dark place stretched for miles. It seemed to be an enormous cavern that probably spread from one side of Dreamland to the other.

"Can't you at least tell us who you are? And why you're taking us away somewhere?" Bill asked softly. "Don't we have a right to know that much?"

"You have whatever rights we give you and no more than that," the bearded man shot back, pointing his finger at Bill. "Don't forget it! Now like I said a while back, you twins do what you're told and nobody will get hurt, see? But if you give us a bad time — well, you can do things the easy way, or the *hard* way! But either way, you're going to do what we tell you to do!"

"But we're just little kids, sir," Barbara responded in her best sweet-little-girl voice. "How could two twelve-year-old children be much benefit to you and your friends? What could we possibly do for you?"

This time, the bearded man laughed a heavy, booming guffaw from deep in his gut. His head bounced up and down and his belly shook as if his shirt were stuffed with Jell-O.

"You'll find out soon enough, little sister," he said, still laughing. "Believe me, you twins will both find out what you can do for us real soon!"

Chapter Ten

Somewhere, a telephone rang.

The bearded man reached into his jacket pocket and pulled out a small cellular phone, switching it on and flipping down the mouthpiece to speak.

Maybe this was a chance, Barbara and Bill both thought. Maybe it was the only chance they had left.

They had both always avoided cell phones. They thought people who used them in restaurants and other public places were rude.

But this was different. If they could find some way to get hold of that phone, they might have an opportunity to call the police for help.

"Yeah, it's me. Who'd ya think was gonna answer this phone, Michael Jordan?" the bearded man said gruffly. "Yeah, that's right. Uh-huh. Yeah, these two would be good for that. They can talk, all right! Man, can they both talk! Yeah, tell him I said so. We'll be right over."

Bill and Barbara watched as the man slid the phone back into his jacket pocket. The twins glanced at each other, each knowing that the other was thinking exactly the same thing.

One of them had to find a way to steal that phone — and hide it until they were alone!

For the time being, though, all they could do was wait, and ride quietly with the bearded man.

Even after traveling so fast for so long, the van still moved swiftly through the underground darkness of the great cavern.

It seemed this black place would never end.

And that the van would drive on forever.

But finally, the van screeched to a halt and the driver opened his mouth for the first time.

"This is it!" he announced in a rough voice.

Before them stood a small brick building, as if someone had constructed a tiny one-bedroom house under Dreamland. Inside the building, many lights burned brightly.

Shadows moved back and forth across the windows.

"OK, kids. *Out!*" the bearded man said, reaching to open the door.

"Where are we?" Bill asked. "What are you going to do with us?"

"I told you — you'll find out soon enough," the man answered. "Now shut up and get going! Both of ya!"

This was their chance, the twins thought. Both of them knew just what they had to do.

Bill began to speak excitedly, waving his arms. At the same time, he slowly walked a few steps to his left, forcing the bearded man to turn with him.

Barbara stood motionless — and waited for the right moment to strike.

"I just can't take any more of this, mister," Bill began, wincing as if he were in pain. "It's my arms, my legs. My whole body hurts! I have diabetes and without my insulin, I'm going to go into shock.

You have to let us go! Don't you see? Don't you see? We have to go home!"

"Listen, kid! I don't care what you have," the bearded man said, turning to watch Bill carefully. "I don't know from diabetes or nothing. I only know I'm supposed to bring you here. And here you are! Now shut up, will ya?"

"No, you don't get it, mister," Bill continued, talking rapidly. "I'm a sick kid. And if I go much longer without my medicine, I'll die! You're going to be a kid killer! And the police will put you in the electric chair for killing a kid! I'm sick! I'm sick! I need help! You have to let us go!"

"Just be quiet!" the bearded man shouted angrily. "Now get inside that building! You and your kid sister, too!"

"She's not my kid sister! We're twins, you idiot," Bill responded, hoping to distract the bearded man by making him angry. "That means we were born at the same time! Boy, you're stupid! Now listen, I'm telling you to get me out of here! Both of us! Or I'm going to die and you'll go to the electric chair!"

As Bill spoke, Barbara moved her hand slowly, slowly, slowly toward the bearded man.

She reached for his jacket pocket — and the cellular phone.

Inch by inch, slowly and more slowly still, as her brother shouted and waved his arms, her hand crept toward the pocket.

Until, at last, her hand was *in* the pocket.

She could feel the cellular phone! Yes, she had it in her hand!

All she had to do was slip it out of the man's pocket and into her own pocket before he noticed.

Little by little, she raised the phone out of the jacket.

Little by little, the twins' hopes of rescue improved.

Then from behind, Barbara heard a loud cough — and a rough voice.

The van driver spoke again.

"Uh, maybe you'd like to know that a little girl almost picked your pocket, you big stupid lug," the driver said to the bearded man. "The kid's right! You *are* dumb! If I hadn't turned my head to look at her, she'd have swiped your cell phone!"

The bearded man whirled around, glared furiously at Barbara and grabbed her hand.

"Ow, you're hurting me," she complained. "Stop it, you're hurting me."

"Leave her alone!" Bill said, tugging at the man's arm. "Leave my sister alone!"

The bearded man picked Bill up by the shirt, grabbing him hard with one hand and twisting Barbara's arm with the other.

"I told ya not to make any trouble, didn't I? I told ya to be good little twins and you wouldn't get hurt," the man shouted. "But you two wouldn't listen! Ya had to try something funny, didn't ya?"

"Look, we're s-sorry, mister," Bill said, wincing with real pain this time. "We didn't m-mean any harm!"

"Well, it's too late for that now, you little twerps," the man hollered. "You tried to make a monkey out of me! And ya know what happens to anyone who tries to make me look stupid? *Do ya?*"

"Uh, n-no, sir," Bill stammered.

"N-no, we don't," Barbara said, her voice trembling.

"I take them in my hand, like this," the man said, shaking both Bill and Barbara hard. "And I shake them until they see things my way! So they won't give no one else any trouble ever again!"

Chapter Eleven

The bearded man wasn't kidding.

Scowling fiercely, he began to shake the Donovan twins even harder.

They were getting dizzy!

He shook them harder and harder. The twins choked and coughed and gagged.

Phwwaaath! Klooowwwck! Gaaaaaaaccchh!

Bill and Barbara kicked and struggled to free themselves from the man's vise-like grip. Gradually, their kicks grew weaker. They simply felt too sick to their stomachs to resist any more. They felt themselves go limp.

They thought they might throw up.

Suddenly, they heard a powerful bass voice.

"Stop it!" someone commanded. "Let them

go!"

Immediately the twins felt the bearded man release them. They fell to the ground in two lumps, panting for breath.

"You ignorant imbecile!" boomed the strong, deep voice. "Do you realize what would have happened to you if you'd actually killed these two? You'd have been finished — for good! They'd have done you in for certain!"

"Well, yeah, I guess you're right," the bearded man agreed. "I just got mad, I guess. The little twerps with their huge noses! Uh, sorry I got so angry, but they tried to steal my phone. Sorry about that, Alex!"

"Do you know how rare these kids are, a pair of cute twins like these?" Alex thundered. "I don't care if they have large noses or not! Now go on! Get back in the van. Both of you get out of here! And don't let me catch you treating our valuable kids that way anymore!"

The twins lay on the floor, starting to get their breath back. Bill rubbed his throat gingerly.

This was all so strange, they thought.

One minute they were being strangled, the next minute someone was talking about them as if they were worth more than gold.

They turned to face Alex, the man with the powerful bass voice — and were surprised to find that he was very short. But he was obviously very strong, like an Olympic weight lifter. He had shoulders as wide as a Volkswagen.

He smiled kindly at the twins and extended his hands to help them up.

"I'm so sorry about all this, kids," he said to them. "Here, brush yourselves off now and come on inside. Let me give you a cold soda pop to soothe your throats. No one will treat you like that again."

"Thank you very much, sir," Barbara said. "It's so nice to meet someone who isn't shouting and screaming at us."

"Yes, or trying to choke us to death,". Bill added.

Alex shook his head sadly.

"I'm so sorry that ever happened," he said.

"You should be given all the courtesies we can extend to you. Come on inside now, please. As my personal guests."

What a sudden change!

Someone actually was treating them nicely. Maybe this whole thing really *was* just a big mistake after all.

Maybe, after their fall, they had been rescued by some tough Dreamland workers who just didn't like kids. And maybe now they were with someone kind, someone kind — and, thank goodness, in charge.

Alex probably would apologize for the entire mess, and take them back to their parents.

For the first time since they had entered the tunnel almost two hours earlier, the Donovan twins smiled.

Yes, everything was just a big mistake, they felt sure. They would be back with Mom and Dad before long.

The small brick building seemed to be Alex's headquarters.

He escorted Bill and Barbara to an office, where they sat in wide, comfortable leather chairs, sipped ice-cold colas, and munched on warm chocolate chip cookies.

Things were going to be all right.

"That's good, kids. You eat all those cookies if you want them," Alex said kindly. "Can I offer you another cola? Or something else to drink?"

"No, thank you, sir," Bill replied. "This tastes great. I was pretty hungry and thirsty after everything we've been through."

"No, I don't want anything else either, sir," Barbara said. "But my brother and I really appreciate your kindness. We were scared to death. And our throats really hurt after what that man did to us."

"Yes, I would think so. Such a crude, foul man," Alex answered softly. "I'm glad you're feeling better now. Maybe, if you're feeling up to it, you both would follow me for a minute. Do you mind? Are you well enough?"

The twins looked at each other and smiled. At last, they were going to leave this huge, dark, terrible cavern beneath Dreamland!

"Yes, sure, we're happy to get out of here," Bill said.

"You lead the way and we'll follow, sir," Barbara said, beaming. "We're fine now, thanks to you."

But Alex didn't lead them out of the cavern — only into another room nearby.

It was packed with electronic equipment: tape recorders and sound boards and microphones and head phones. Cassette tapes littered the tables and spilled on to the floor.

The room looked like a recording studio, the twins thought. Why would Alex bring them in there?

Where was the exit that would take them outside, back up to Dreamland and their waiting, worried parents?

"Excuse me, but I don't understand," Bill said. "Do you need us to make some kind of statement on tape about what happened to us? We're really tired and want to get back to Mom and Dad. But I *guess* we could give you a statement before we go — right, Barbara?"

"Sure, I guess so," she said reluctantly. "But I really don't understand why we have to do this now. We just want to return to Dreamland and see our parents now, please."

Alex smiled gently, like an understanding uncle.

"I guess there's some confusion here, kids," he said. "I'll try to explain it to you. You see, kids, you *are* in Dreamland. In fact, this is the most important part of this whole big theme park."

"Huh? What do you mean?" Bill asked. "I don't get it."

"Yes, that doesn't make any sense," Barbara added.

"You'll understand more about it as we go along. It'll all become clear quite soon," Alex said softly, smiling. "And as for seeing your parents, well I wouldn't worry about that, if I were you two. Because you kids are going to be staying as our guests in Dreamland for a while. Yes, in fact, you're going to be staying here for a long time."

He paused, looked them over, and smiled more broadly.

" Long enough," he said, "that you'll never see your parents again!"

Chapter Twelve

Never see their parents again?

Alex's words sent shudders of terror through Bill and Barbara.

"Sir, I, uh, m-m-may not have heard you right j-just now," Bill stammered. "W-what did you say?"

"I said, you're going to stay with us at Dreamland for a long time," Alex said, still smiling. "And I'm afraid you won't be able to see your parents again."

Overcome with fear, Barbara screamed as loudly as she could.

Aaaaaaaaahhhh!

Bill felt like screaming too, but he didn't.

"Shhhh, shhhh now," Alex said quietly. "Getting hysterical won't help anything. No one can hear you."

They stared at him in horror.

He looked back at them kindly.

"I'm sure all this is something of a shock to you both," he said. "But you see, we need you for our work here. You're very important to Dreamland."

"We don't want to be important," Bill shot back. "We want to go home!"

"But, listen, son," Alex said. "Isn't it every child's fantasy to come to Dreamland? Think how many children tell their parents, 'I wish I never had to leave Dreamland!' We're granting you two the fondest request any kid could ever make. To stay forever in Dreamland!"

"We never said we didn't want to leave Dreamland," Bill said angrily. "We have no intention of staying with you. And don't ever call me 'son' again! I'm not your son!"

"We're not staying here a minute longer!" Barbara said, recovering her wits. "Come along, Bill! We're going!"

In an attempt to bluff their way out of this kidnapping, Bill and Barbara straightened their backs and walked with determination toward the door.

Alex stepped in front of them and blocked their path. Gently, he took hold of their arms.

"Kids, kids, kids! I have to admire your courage. But I'm afraid we can't let you go," he said with a smile.

"I don't understand this," Barbara said, beginning to cry.

Bill fought back tears, too.

"What do you want us for, mister?" Barbara asked. "Why do we have to stay in Dreamland forever?"

"As I said, we have some very special work for you," Alex said. "And that work begins right here — in this room. Right now."

Bill and Barbara looked at each other. They had tried to escape and failed. There seemed nothing to do but bide their time and comply with Alex's orders while hoping for another chance.

Alex led them to a large microphone and put

a pair of headphones on each of them. He handed them a sheet of paper with neatly printed dialogue on it.

This is what it said:

Boy: Jane, I'm having the time of my life in Dreamland! It's so great to finally see this place after hearing about it from my friends!

Girl: It's just the coolest, Tom! I can't wait to get home and tell everyone about it!

Boy: Yeah, except I don't want to leave Dreamland! (Boy laughs.) It's got the best, most incredible rides in the world! Everything seems so real — it's hard to believe it's just pretend!

Girl: I know, Tom! In The Man in the Moon, I felt just like I was really flying in space!

Boy: Yeah, and in The Haunting House, I felt like the place was really possessed by evil spirits! Wow, was that great or what?

Girl: There's no way around it, Tom. Every kid has got to come to Dreamland at least once! (Girl laughs.) It's the best place in the world! Once you get here, you never want to leave!"

Bill and Barbara read the words with puzzled expressions on their faces.

"You want us to read this? Why? I don't understand, mister," Bill said.

"Why should we do some sort of commercial for this place when we've been treated so badly?" Barbara said.

"Because, kids, I'm telling you to do it," Alex said softly. "And here in Dreamland, you do what I tell you to do."

"Or *what*?" Bill asked.

"Or," Alex answered with a gentle smile, "you both die."

Chapter Thirteen

"Now after I count to three, I'll point at you," Alex explained. "And then you start talking, son. Then it's your turn, honey. And back and forth through the copy, all right?"

"I'm *not* your son!" Bill said.

"And don't call me 'honey!' " Barbara said. "Why don't you at least call us by our names?"

"Because kids, I don't know your names and I don't want to," Alex replied. "Now just do as you're told! We need some good, believable voices for these radio ads. We've found that it's best to use the same voices that kids will later hear in person inside the park."

"What do you mean by that?" Bill asked. "What do you mean the same voices kids will hear in the park?"

"Let's not get ahead of ourselves," Alex said with a laugh. "You'll find out about all that later. Just focus on reading your lines correctly, all right, kids?"

But reading their lines correctly turned out to be very difficult for the twins, even though both were excellent readers, whether reading out loud to others or silently to themselves.

They just couldn't concentrate because they were so nervous, so worried, so frightened by what had happened to them.

Time after time, one or the other mispronounced a word. They couldn't make themselves chuckle when their parts called for laughs.

Through all of this, Alex was extremely patient.

"That's OK. Just try it again," he kept saying softly.

Finally, after an hour of mistakes, the twins read their lines properly, even getting the phony laughs right.

Bill and Barbara would make fine actors!

At least, that's what Alex told them.

"We're not actors at all," Barbara said. "We're just kids. And we want to go home. Can't you let us go now?"

"Yeah, mister. We want to see our parents now," Bill added. "We've done what you wanted us to do. Why don't you just let us out of here and we'll never tell anyone a thing about it. We just want to leave. We don't want to be actors."

"Well, you had *better* want to become actors," Alex said with a smile. "Because that's what you're both going to do. You two are going to be famous."

"You must be crazy, mister," Bill said. "How could we become famous?"

"What do you mean by saying something so strange?" Barbara asked. "Why would we become famous? Besides, even if we did get famous someday, we'd probably become famous musicians, not actors."

"*Musicians*!" Alex exclaimed. "Perfect! You play instruments then, do you?"

"Yes, we do," Bill said. "So what?"

"I play the clarinet. My brother plays the oboe," Barbara announced. "We're both considered very talented, even if I do say so myself!"

"That's just wonderful, kids! Marvelous! Even better than having you speak lines," Alex said, beaming. "You'll fit in perfectly! Now you can be musicians all you like — *and* actors, too! Right here at Dreamland!"

"You keep saying we're going to be actors," Bill said. "But we're not. Neither my sister nor I have any intention of becoming actors. Not *ever*!"

"Well, that's where you're quite wrong, son," Alex said, smiling. "Because in about one hour, both you and your sister are going to become actors who will be seen by millions of people! Each of you will have a great part — and you will get to act in that one role for the rest of your lives!"

Chapter Fourteen

"Come with me!" Alex said. "We're going to take another little ride through Dreamland."

Holding each of them by the hand, he walked the Donovans out of the recording studio and down a short hallway to a small wooden door.

The door creaked when he opened it, like one that might have been in The Haunting House.

Bill and Barbara found themselves looking down a long, dark stairway. It looked like a stairway to the very center of the earth.

"OK, kids, let's go!" Alex said happily. "Down the steps we go. You first, son. You go after him, honey. I'll stay behind you."

The twins looked at each other in horror.

Where were they going now? What terrible

thing was going to happen to them next?

Cautiously, slowly, step by step, Bill began to descend the stairs. His legs shook with fear.

Behind him, Barbara walked even more slowly, her legs trembling just as hard.

The stairs began to curl around in a tight loop, spiraling down into the blackness, winding around and around, around and around.

There seemed no end to them.

"Mister, do we have to go down here with you?" Barbara asked, her voice weak. She felt tears form in her eyes. "This is just awful."

"Yeah, I don't s-see why we need to g-go way down here," Bill said with a frightened stutter.

"I know, I know. It's a terrible staircase, isn't it?" Alex said sympathetically. "I don't enjoy it much myself, kids. But just keep going. Please. We're almost there now."

On and on, on and on, on and on, the stairs swirled down and down into the dark below.

At last, Bill's foot touched solid ground.

He saw a single headlight inside a tunnel to

his right. The headlight was coming nearer.

"Where are we?" Bill asked. "Where are we going?"

"Can't you tell us *something*? Please!" Barbara begged. "You're frightening us to death!"

"I'm afraid you'll just have to wait a little longer," Alex said. "It's going to be a big surprise for you both. And that's all I can say for now."

The twins could see that the headlight was part of a small train that was approaching at high speed. As the train neared, Bill and Barbara saw that it had a single engine — with only one tiny car attached.

The car had enough room for six or seven people. No more than that.

With Alex guiding them by their hands, the twins reluctantly climbed aboard the train.

It took off the moment they sat down.

The train sped off at a blistering pace. Both twins understood at once that this must be a special, underground version of Dreamland's Bullet Train.

They paid attention to the direction the train

was traveling, hoping to determine whether they were heading back toward The Haunting House — or farther still from the last place they had seen their parents.

The train made a long, wide arc to the right, as if reversing its original direction. Without a word between them, the twins both reached the same conclusion: The train probably was going back toward The Haunting House.

It was hard to tell for sure, especially after that confusing, winding trip down the long stairway.

But they both guessed that the speeding train was taking them closer to where they wanted to be.

They hoped desperately they were right!

Perhaps fifteen minutes later, the train came to a long, squealing halt in the darkness. Apparently they had reached another subterranean station, somewhere in the bowels of the world's most famous theme park.

"All right, kids, this is the place," Alex said. The train doors opened.

Holding their hands, Alex escorted the Donovans toward a big building, a place that seemed to be brightened by ten-thousand lights blazing in its many windows. It looked like a massive office building that had been constructed a mile below the earth's surface.

"Wow!" Bill said, impressed in spite of himself. "What is this place?"

"I've never seen anything like it," Barbara said, her mouth hanging open. "Even in a movie. This is incredible!"

"Yes, it is incredible, isn't it kids?" Alex said proudly. "It's like no other place in the world. A scientific facility that is unique in all the history of humankind!"

"A scientific facility? You mean all this is just a lab?" Barbara asked.

"A lab and much, much more, honey," Alex said enthusiastically. "It is a monument to brilliant ingenuity! A temple to enshrine the genius of Dreamland! It is a technical achievement that makes all the marvels of modern medicine, all the miracles of space travel seem like child's play! It is a place of *extraordinary* powers wielded by *human beings*!"

He gazed at the building and gestured toward it for emphasis.

"It is," he said, *"the eighth wonder of the world!"*

"What is it, mister?" Bill said, interrupting impatiently. "We don't know what you're talking about."

"I'm talking about science, child. Science as it is practiced no where else on this or any other planet," Alex said, his mouth almost foaming from excitement.

"Our scientists have invented a process so remarkable that no one would believe it — even if we announced the truth on every TV network in the world!" he said. "Even experts would say it's impossible. But here it is — standing before your own eyes! It is the very essence of Dreamland! Most ordinary theme parks try to make fantasy seem close to reality. But here, in the greatest theme park of all, we turn *reality* into *fantasy*! *That* is the genius of Dreamland, children!"

"Can't you just tell us what you mean by all of this?" Barbara said. "We're scared and confused — and you're just making things worse."

"Then let me put it simply, kids," Alex said, smiling gently again. "This is Dreamland's animatronics center."

He paused, as if trying to think of the best way to explain.

"It's where our great robots are created," he said. "It's where we make all the incredibly lifelike kids and adults and animals you see all over Dreamland, robots so believable that you can't tell them from real people and animals. Robots that look just like real-life robbers and cowboys and soldiers, like waiters and cooks and janitors, like giraffes and crocodiles and buffalo and a thousand other things!"

"What's the big deal about that?" Bill asked. "Every theme park has some place where they make their robot people and animals and stuff. Yeah, sure — Dreamland's robots are a lot better. But I wouldn't call the lab that makes your robots the eighth wonder of the world."

"Ah, but it *is* the eighth wonder of the world," Alex said, getting excited again as he stared at the bright building surrounded by blackness.

"Because it's the place where we take *real people* and *real animals* and turn them into Dreamland robots," he said. "And it's the place where we're taking both of you!"

"What?" Bill exclaimed, shocked.

"What?" Barbara cried, terrified.

"Yes, kids, that's right," Alex said.

He was almost trembling with pride. His lips quivered. His eyes shone with excitement.

"You twins will have the great honor of being processed through our brilliant animatronics center!" he exclaimed. "I'm going to take you inside that building and our scientists will perform some tests. Then, they will coat your skin in plastic and give you something to swallow! And you both will exist from that moment on as two of the great living robots of Dreamland!"

Chapter Fifteen

Inside the great, horrible laboratory of Dreamland, Alex walked the Donovans to a small white room.

Everything in it was white: the carpet, the drapes, the furniture, the lamps.

Alex told the twins to sit with him on the long white couch and wait quietly. Almost numb from fear, Bill and Barbara did as they were told.

Tears streaked silently down their cheeks.

They were going to be turned into robots! Living robots!

How could this be happening? The twins felt as if they had become part of a bad science fiction movie.

A tall, skinny man in a long white coat

walked into the room and greeted Alex cordially. He turned and shook hands with Bill and Barbara.

"These two are wonderful specimens!" the skinny man said.

He eyed the Donovans up and down, seeming pleased with what he saw.

"Just marvelous, Alex!" he said. "We have needed a good set of twins about this age for some time now. I'm very pleased!"

"Thank you, Dr. Ferret!" Alex said, smiling. "I'm glad you think they will work out. I'm sure you've been told that they play instruments. The clarinet for the girl, the oboe for the boy. That may help you, too."

"Oh, *yes*! It's just perfect! Just absolutely perfect," Dr. Ferret said, clapping his hands joyfully. "I understand the girl says they play their instruments very well, too. You've done fine work this time, Alex."

"I appreciate that, Dr. Ferret. Thank you again," Alex said, walking toward the door. "Good-bye, kids! I'll be seeing you sometime after you officially take up residence in Dreamland."

"Yes, you'll see them again, Alex," Dr. Ferret said. "They'll be working at The Opera House, playing in the orchestra. If they're as good as the girl says, they'll be featured musicians there — famous animatronics soloists."

After Alex left, Dr. Ferret closely examined the twins, as if they were two white mice ready for some twisted experiment.

"Follow me, children," Dr. Ferret said. "We'll give you new names later, something that will suit your work in the orchestra. Maybe names like Bruno and Helga. Yes, I rather like that! But for now, you'll just be known as 'the twins,' all right?"

Dr. Ferret took the twins down a long hallway with windows on each side. The windows looked into small labs where strange work was underway.

In one lab, large monkeys were tied down on tables as workers injected something into their thin, hairy arms.

In another lab, a huge hippopotamus stood

motionless while a nurse measured the beast, as if for a suit of clothes.

In still another lab, three teenage boys lay stretched out in dentists' chairs, their arms and legs strapped in place. A doctor was forcing the boys to swallow large white pills.

The sight of all this almost made Barbara pass out. Bill felt like he was going to throw up.

Somehow they kept walking with Dr. Ferret, hoping someone might still rescue them before something awful happened, something irreversibly ghastly.

At the end of the long hallway, Dr. Ferret pushed a button and a sliding door opened. He nudged the twins inside, then closed the door by touching another button.

At that moment, Bill and Barbara both realized they had to snap out of their dazed panic if they wanted to survive.

Somehow, they had to be brave and strong.

Most of all, they had to start using their heads!

Bill glanced sideways at his sister, who glanced sideways at him. And each understood.

They had to work together, looking for some way out of this nightmare.

But how?

It seemed so hopeless.

Then in an instant, it came to her.

Barbara had a plan! A desperate plan to escape!

A last-ditch plan that simply *had* to succeed before the Donovans were turned into human zombies!

Chapter Sixteen

Barbara knew that, if her plan was going to work, Dr. Ferret had to leave Bill and her in a room alone for at least half an hour.

And somehow they had to get hold of a clarinet and an oboe to take into that room.

To get all that, they would need to invent some believable lie.

The best way to come up with that lie, Barbara decided, was to begin asking lots of questions — and so gain useful information about the animatronics process.

"Uh, Dr. Ferret, sir," she said in her sweet-little-girl voice. "I'm glad you and Alex are so pleased with my brother and me. We've both decided that it would be nice to stay at Dreamland and play in your Opera House orchestra. But we were wondering — will it hurt to have our skin coated with plastic?"

Bill looked at her. He knew she was up to something but didn't know exactly what.

"No, no, no. Not at all, child," Dr. Ferret answered. "We're not barbarians here. There's no pain during any part of the process."

"But, well, I was wondering how that process works, sir," Barbara said.

"It's quite simple, dear," Dr. Ferret began. "Over a period of three days, we run a series of medical tests on you and your brother. Nothing that will hurt in any way, I promise."

He smiled, evidently pleased that she was taking such an interest in the process.

"We enter data from those tests into our computers," he continued. "And then a special computer program tells us what mixture of plastic will best suit your skin."

"It sounds pretty complicated, sir," Bill observed politely, playing along with Barbara. "Can you tell us a little more? Just so we can be less afraid when the time comes to go through the process."

"Certainly, child," Dr. Ferret said. "I have developed a method to put many thin coats of plastic over the skin, one at a time. The plastic has tiny holes so that your skin can breathe normally. Over a period of one week, your entire body will be given forty-seven coats of plastic — until you look and feel like a very lifelike robot."

"But after the people and animals are coated with plastic, how do you get them to do exactly what you want?" Barbara inquired innocently. "How do you get them to behave like robots, saying or doing the same things over and over?"

"That was one of the most difficult parts of our process at Dreamland," Dr. Ferret explained.

"My research team has come up with a diet of pills that give the body all the necessary nutrients — and yet also make a human being, or even an animal, completely obedient," he said. "We can make a living creature repeat any action it was able to perform before arriving at Dreamland."

"I don't really understand what you mean, sir," Bill interrupted.

"For example, we can't make a Dreamland giraffe talk," Dr. Ferret said patiently. "That's because real giraffes don't talk. But we can make a Dreamland giraffe reach up and eat tree leaves every five seconds, endlessly. Or we can instruct a soldier to run over a Dreamland battlefield every minute, in the same way, all day long."

"So the pills let you program people and animals, almost like you program computers?" Barbara wondered sweetly.

"Yes, that's it exactly," Dr. Ferret said. "As long as we keep feeding our robots their pills every day, they will do anything they're told to do."

He beamed at them with pride.

"In your case," he said, "you twins will be shown how to play three or four pieces of music. Then you'll play the same pieces of music for every Dreamland audience at The Opera House, all day long. Day after day, forever."

Dr. Ferret grinned triumphantly.

"And you'll play the music in exactly the same way during every performance," he said. "You'll never get tired. And you'll never need water or food during the day."

"As long as we keep taking those pills, you mean. Right, Dr. Ferret?" Bill asked.

"Yes, that's right, child. But you won't have to worry about missing any of your pills," Dr. Ferret explained. "We make absolutely certain that each Dreamland robot gets just the right mixture of pills each night before sleeping, without fail. Then that robot is re-programmed to perform its task when the park opens the following morning."

"But one thing concerns me, Dr. Ferret," Barbara said, with a quick look at her brother. "We haven't had any chance to practice our instruments for several days now. We've been on vacation. And I'm afraid we're very rusty. So when you program us to play your music, it won't sound very good."

"That's true, Dr. Ferret," Bill agreed. "Our skills deteriorate if we don't practice every day."

"So we were just wondering if you could get

us the clarinet and oboe you'll want us to use in the orchestra," Barbara suggested. "Then maybe you can find a room where we could practice our instruments, just for a little while before we take your pills."

"Yes, if you let us practice, we'll sound great for your Opera House audiences," Bill said. "That way, we can be featured musicians, just as you want. But we really will need to practice alone somewhere."

"Even a half hour of practice would help. But we need privacy so we can concentrate — and also so we won't disturb your lab employees," Barbara added.

All this puzzled Dr. Ferret.

No one selected for the animatronics process had ever asked him to practice anything before taking the pills.

But the request seemed logical enough, he finally decided. After all, the girl had a good point: If the twins couldn't play their best *before* they were programmed, they couldn't play their best *after* programming either.

A little practice certainly couldn't hurt anything.

So Dr. Ferret picked up a phone in the lab and asked an assistant to bring him an oboe and a clarinet from the Dreamland prop department.

Then Dr. Ferret gave Bill and Barbara their new instruments and ushered them into a small room beside the lab, instructing them to practice.

"I'll be working right here in the laboratory while you play, children," Dr. Ferret said as he locked the door. "I'm afraid I can only give you a half hour. We have many medical tests to run on you twins. I hope that time will help. I'll be listening to you, so practice your instruments nicely for me, please."

As soon as they were alone in the secluded little room, Bill whispered to his twin sister.

"What's this all about, sis?" he asked. "I knew you were trying to get us away from that madman for a while. And then I figured out that you wanted to get instruments for us to play. But why?"

"Because I have a plan to escape while we

still have the chance," Barbara explained quickly. "In the recording studio, when Alex wasn't looking, I stole this tape recorder. I thought it might help us get away somehow."

Barbara pulled a small, black tape recorder from her pants pocket.

"That's great, sis," Bill said. "But what good will a tape recorder do us now?"

"Look, Bill — we'll play our instruments for a while and let the tape recorder run. Then while we escape through this window here, we'll play the tape of our practice session," Barbara said. "Dr. Ferret will think we're still rehearsing. By the time the tape runs out, we'll be gone."

"Brilliant! Just brilliant!" Bill whispered. "I knew my sister was a genius, but this plan is just spectacular."

Barbara turned on the tape recorder as Bill began to practice his oboe.

He played scales in the keys of A, B-flat, D and G minor. Then Barbara began to play, scales and melodies in the keys of C and F-sharp.

Together, they created a terrible racket! And that was just what they wanted to do.

After a few minutes, Barbara rewound the tape to the beginning as Bill continued to blow into his oboe.

She pushed the machine's play button.

It worked!

The same terrible racket filled the little room, just as if Bill and Barbara were still practicing.

Now they had to work fast. Very fast!

The tape recording would last only about ten minutes. After that, there would be a sudden silence — and Dr. Ferret would surely open the door to see what was going on.

The twins hurried to the room's only window, a ground floor window that looked into the dark underground train station.

They planned to break it with their instruments while the recorded music blared into the room.

Then they would run along the railroad tracks, searching for some way out of the huge cavern beneath Dreamland.

Except now there was a new problem.

A very serious problem.

The window wouldn't break!

It was very strong glass — probably bullet-proof.

It was certainly oboe-proof and clarinet-proof! No matter how hard they swung their instruments against the glass, the window would not break.

Wildly, the twins groped around the room for some other way to escape.

There was nothing — no other door, no other window.

No way out at all!

Only a few minutes of recorded music remained. Bill and Barbara looked at each other with helpless terror in their eyes.

They were trapped inside the home of Dreamland's mad scientists.

And the maddest scientist of all was about to work on them in his laboratory!

Chapter Seventeen

"What are we going to do?" cried Barbara, her hands fluttering around like panicked birds.

"There must be *some* way to get out of this room!" Bill said with determination.

He glanced around quickly.

"Wait, Barbara! Look!" he whispered. "An air duct! Maybe . . . Yes, it's probably just big enough for us to crawl through. Let me see if I can get the cover off."

There in the wall, beside the door, was a vent to carry air conditioning into the room. It was small — very small.

But Bill knew it was their only hope.

Working quickly, he pulled the cover off and squeezed inside. There was just barely enough room to move.

"Come on, Barbara. Follow me!" he said. "We've got to go — right now!"

"I can't crawl through another tunnel, Bill! I just *can't*!" Barbara whined. "Not after what happened to us at The Haunting House! And this one is even smaller than that one was! I couldn't stand it again!"

"Yes, you can!" Bill said sternly.

Still, Barbara did not move. Bill decided that, if he made her angry, maybe then she would follow him.

"Now come on, Babs! Stop being a baby!" he hissed. "We have to be calm at a time like this! The tape recorder is almost through playing our practice session. Come on — right this minute, Babs!"

It worked!

Barbara turned red with anger, just as her mother sometimes did. Without thinking, she climbed into the tiny vent.

"Fine! If we get killed this time by crawling around in a tunnel, it's *your fault*!" she said.

"Just grab the cover and close it behind you, Babs!" Bill ordered. "That way, it may take Dr. Ferret longer to figure out where we went."

Bill and Barbara crawled through the narrow, dark air-conditioning vent. Cold air blew through it. The metal walls of the vent were icy cold to the touch. Their fingers started to get numb.

Shaking and shivering, they crawled as rapidly as their hands and knees could carry them — hands and knees that were still sore from their long crawl through The Haunting House.

"Come on, Babs! Stay up with me," Bill said. "We've got to get out of this place before they know we're gone!"

The ventilation tunnel led them along the outside wall of the animatronics center, to a darkened office in the rear of the building.

Bill peered through the vent cover into the room.

He saw no one there.

Slowly and carefully, he pushed the cover off and the twins crawled out.

There in front of them was a large office window. Bill ran to it, grabbed the sash and tried to slide the window open.

It stuck. Barbara ran to his side and helped lift with all her might. The two of them grunted and strained.

"OK," Bill said. "On three. One . . . two . . . three!"

The two of them shoved the window frame upward as hard as they could.

The window opened!

Bill helped Barbara climb outside, then quickly followed her.

Then the Donovans ran faster than they had ever realized they could run!

They raced through the huge underground train station for what seemed like miles. They gasped for air, but fear made their legs tireless, and they ran on and on without stopping.

At last they saw an iron staircase leading upward. And just maybe, leading outdoors!

In the distance, they heard a loud alarm ring

furiously.

They knew Dr. Ferret had discovered their escape. The Dreamland thugs would be sent out to hunt them down.

Bill and Barbara flew up the staircase. Their muscles burned, but up and up they ran. There would be time enough to rest if they ever managed to escape.

The stairs led to a large wooden door. Bill pushed on it.

The door was jammed! He could budge it open only an inch or two. It seemed that no one had used this doorway in a long time.

"Come up here, Barbara! I need help," Bill said. "Push on this door with me! Maybe together we can force it open!"

They pushed furiously on the door with their shoulders — and finally, it burst open.

They were outside again.

They were free!

It was nighttime but they could see the dim outline of trees and the bright moon and the sparkling stars. What a wonderful feeling to be away from that terrible cavern under Dreamland!

But the twins understood they were not safe yet — far from it!

They had to find their parents again. Or at least find someone who didn't work at Dreamland, some tourist who could protect them and bring them to the police.

"Look, Bill!" Barbara shouted with excitement. "The Dreamland parking area is just over there! I can't see very well because it's so dark, but the parking lot doesn't look too far away! Maybe Mom and Dad are waiting for us at the car!"

"You're right, Barbara. Parking space PH36! I almost forgot about that," Bill said. "Let's run that way! Quickly, before someone from Dreamland sees us!"

The twins tore across the open field toward the parking lot.

Before they even got there, they stopped dead!

Because now they could see something they

hadn't noticed from farther away. The parking lot was empty.

Completely empty!

Including parking space PH36!

Not one car in sight anywhere.

No worried parents waiting patiently by the four-door rental car.

Even worse, they saw two men hurrying across the parking lot.

And they recognized them. The bearded man and one of his assistants strode quickly across the lot, directly toward them!

"Hurry, Barbara!" Bill yelled. "This way, back the way we came! Back to the field!"

But it was too late for that.

Two other men were running toward the twins from the field. There could not escape that way.

Two more men ran at them from their right! Two more from their left!

The twins were surrounded by Dreamland's goon squad, including some of the same thugs who had captured them under The Haunting House.

Bill and Barbara looked at each other with expressions of pure horror.

It was all over for them this time.

And no amount of clever, quick thinking could do anything to change their fate!

Chapter Eighteen

Barbara grabbed Bill and held on tightly.

What else could she do now?

Maybe somehow if she hugged her brother long enough, all the bad things would stop.

Bill felt just as afraid — and hugged his sister just as tightly.

The twins shuddered as the thugs closed in. This time, the end really was at hand.

They were trapped by kidnappers who worked for the most insane scientists in the world.

Then, suddenly, they heard a strange noise.

What was it, they wondered. Bill and Barbara looked at each other with puzzled faces.

Kaa-whack! Kaa-whack! Kaa-whack! Kaa-whack! Kaa-whack!

It was a helicopter, and the noise came from the beating of the large chopper's huge propellers.

The chopper swooped low over them, its spotlight cutting through the moonlit darkness. Bill and Barbara began to shout and jump up and down and wave their arms wildly.

Because this was a police helicopter!

Alerted by Mr. and Mrs. Donovan shortly after the twins' disappearance, the police had immediately launched a search of the area around Dreamland.

"We've had other reports of missing persons at Dreamland," one police captain had told the frantic parents. "Nothing we could pin down because often it's been adults, and we never heard about the missing people until a day or two after they disappeared. But your kids haven't been gone that long — and we're going to find them. And maybe find out what's going on at Dreamland, too."

All state and local officers in the Orlando area had been called in to start a massive hunt for the missing twins.

And now, two chopper cops had found them!

The chopper circled and swooped over the children again, very low this time!

The helicopter hovered over the Donovans, shining the spotlight directly on them.

"This is the police!" a loudspeaker in the chopper announced. "Remain calm and don't move! Wait right there! You'll be all right! We'll land to pick you up in a moment!"

But first, the helicopter would chase away the Dreamland thugs, who were scattering wildly in all directions.

The police followed the bearded man, who sprinted away as fast as his fat body allowed. It wasn't nearly fast enough.

"Stop! This is the police!" the chopper loudspeaker called to him. "You are under arrest!"

At that instant, dozens of police cars rushed in from every side, sirens blaring, blue lights flashing. Maybe a hundred police officers spread out over the field and parking lot, scouring the area for the kidnappers.

Within minutes, every thug was captured. Soon afterward, the chopper returned for Bill and Barbara.

They really were safe at last, rescued just in time by the police!

"Are you OK, kids?" one chopper cop asked, helping them aboard. "Your parents were worried to death! They were sure something terrible had happened."

"Something terrible *did* happen," Barbara answered. "And it's *still* happening right now — to lots of other kids. And even a lot of adults, too!"

"You're not going to believe this story, sir. But I swear, it's all true!" Bill said.

During the short flight back to the police station, Bill and Barbara told the officers their incredible tale of the bearded man and Alex and Dr. Ferret — and the underground lab that turned people into living robots.

One of the policemen began to take careful notes.

The chopper slowly descended to the police

station landing pad.

The moment the helicopter landed, Mr. and Mrs. Donovan rushed to meet their children, kissing them and hugging them as if they had been gone for ten years instead of ten hours.

"Thank God, you're both safe!" Mr. Donovan said.

"Thank you so much for rescuing our children!" Mrs. Donovan told the officers.

The chopper cops smiled, but hurried off. They rushed into the police chief's office, informing him all about the horrors of Dreamland.

With Bill and Barbara's help, the Orlando police, the Florida Highway Patrol and the FBI all began an immediate investigation.

Before the theme park could open for tourists the next morning, the authorities had shut it down for good.

They arrested everyone involved with Dreamland, from the bearded man to Alex to Dr. Ferret.

A special team of physicians freed the living

robots from their plastic skins and fed them solid food and lots of water — and waited until Dr. Ferret's pills wore off.

Within two days, all the children and adults who had become slaves were walking and talking, laughing and crying normally again. They were human beings with wills of their own, not zombies under the power of twisted, greedy minds.

Bill and Barbara Donovan were hailed as heroes, even though both insisted they really weren't.

"We were just trying to save ourselves," Bill said. "We were luckier than a lot of the other people who were kidnapped at Dreamland, that's all."

Luckier, yes. And just maybe, a little smarter as well.

Smart enough to outsmart the brilliant and terrible Dr. Ferret.

And smart enough to understand that they wouldn't have survived Dreamland without each other, without the combined brains and strength and courage and love they shared.

After their ordeal, Bill and Barbara felt closer

to each other than ever.

They agreed to treasure this special relationship all their lives, the relationship of a brother and sister who understood each other and trusted each other and cared for each other very much.

As they flew home to Detroit from Orlando with their parents, Bill and Barbara agreed on something else, too.

"Mom and Dad, I have a good idea," Bill began with a grin. "Let's go to Orlando again sometime. It could be a really great place to take a vacation. But next time . . ."

Barbara looked at her brother, smiled — and finished his sentence. Once again, the twins were thinking exactly the same thing.

"Next time," Barbara said with a laugh, "let's go to Disney World!"